CELEBRATE STORIES. LOVE READING.

PATRICE LAWRENCE

SNAP

Hodder
Children's
Books

HODDER CHILDREN'S BOOKS

First published in Great Britain in 2019 by Hodder and Stoughton

1 3 5 7 9 10 8 6 4 2

A CIP catalogue record for this book is available from the British Library.

ISBN 978 1 444 95020 5

ISBN (Export) 978 1 444 95019 9

Printed and bound in Great Britain by CPI (UK) Ltd, Croydon, CR0 4YY

The paper and board used in this book are from well-managed forests
and other responsible sources.

Hodder Children's Books
An imprint of Hachette Children's Group
Part of Hodder & Stoughton
Carmelite House
50 Victoria Embankment
London EC4Y 0DZ

An Hachette UK Company
www.hachette.co.uk

www.hachettechildrens.co.uk

Squad

'The boy said I had a face like a lemming.'

Reba's in full flow, the squad all gathered round her. They've got their mouths open like they want to taste her words as well as hear them. It's a full-on bedroom takeover. Jeans and sweatshirts are heaped on my bed and someone's spilled liquid foundation over my rug. It must be Kim's. She's the only one who matches that colour.

Kim says, 'What's a lemming?'

5

Reba rolls her eyes so hard I can hear her lashes slap her forehead. 'They're like meerkats, but cuter.'

I say, 'You sure it's a compliment? He thinks your face is small and furry, right?'

Reba sucks her teeth. 'You wouldn't know a compliment if it bounced off your belly, Soraya. What the boy's saying is that my face is so sweet, he'd follow it over a cliff.'

Kim's looking really confused.

Sobia fills her in. 'Lemmings are supposed to follow each other, no matter what.'

Kim shrieks. 'That's stupid! If you fall off a cliff, you'll both be dead! Who wants to be dead?'

There's silence. Even the damn music stops, like Kendrick's paused it himself to see what I'll do next. Kim catches the mood late and looks around. Her mouth's open even wider, like she's expecting to catch really big words in there. Boy, I almost give them to her, all the giant, angry words that have been bouncing round our house for the last two weeks. Instead, Reba clears her throat and Kim catches her eye and claps her hand over her mouth.

'Damn, Soraya! Sorry!'

I make a point of looking around my destroyed bedroom, but don't say nothing. After all, they're doing me a favour by being here at all.

I say, 'Y'all ready?'

They nod.

'And y'all know the way?'

They nod again.

'Okay. Time to go.'

I leave them to pack up their things and I go down to Dad. He's still in his big armchair like somebody's stapled him there. Farhad's on the sofa, squirmy as usual. G-Gran used to shake her head at Dad: *Lewis, God lace your boy's pants with cow itch, or somet'ing?* She was right. Farhad's always been twitchy. I think he's got so many thoughts he runs out of space in his head so they have to zoom up and down the rest of his body. He's wearing a suit. It looks black because Dad's drawn the curtains even though it's still light. I know the suit's dark grey. It's the one Dad made him wear to work experience.

I can hear the girls coming down the stairs. There's a giggle. That must be Kim. She can never hold it in. Dad looks up and my stomach hurts. I know how he's gonna see them. I know what he's gonna feel about them. I just want him to know I tried to get it right.

Reba comes in first. She's wearing heels you could murder someone with. I push that thought right to the back of my head. Her trousers are tight and black, slashed so you can see her leg underneath, with a top that can't quite meet her waistband. If she reaches up, everyone's gonna see her belly, but at least her sleeves cover her Groot tattoo. Kim's wearing the longest dress I ever seen her in. It reaches right down to her knees. She's got the colour right, but her big disc earrings could pick up cable and her lipstick's so dark it looks like she's yawning. Sobia's got her headscarf on, though as far as I remember, she stopped wearing it three years ago. She gives me a nervous smile. Out of all of them, she's never done nothing like this before and she's made the best go – a black maxi skirt with trainers underneath and a jumper. I nod back, letting her know she's all right.

Dad's eyes skid past Sobia to Kim to Reba. He frowns and pushes his lips together. Then he stands up.

'Farhad,' he says. 'Let's go to Jimi-Luke.'

Farhad sort of flings himself off the sofa. As he pulls his hand out his trouser pocket, I see something gold slither through his fingers and disappear. Mum's chain. I feel a little better. He'd found it when we were clearing out the old place before we moved here. He used to wear it all the time, but just recently his neck's been bare. When I asked him if he'd lost it, he got a mood on, so I didn't bother again. I'm glad he's found it. He's always believed in good luck charms.

We're gonna need it.

Precious

Jimi-Luke's my uncle, though he's only a couple of years older than me. I only met him once. It wasn't even a proper meeting. He passed by our house, had a big shout-off with Dad and stormed away again. He'd got himself in trouble and he wanted Dad to help him. Dad said 'no'.

Dad keeps the car windows rolled up high. I'm in the front and I can feel Farhad behind me. He's just stillness. I want the cold to come in. I want to feel sharp and awake, but no way am I going to go against Dad and push that window-down button. He's muttering about where to park and I don't say what I want to say. *We don't have to do this, Dad. The cars would have come to our house.*

We find a back street and me and Farhad escape from Dad's stress and wait on the pavement while he checks there's no parking regs. If he gets another ticket, there'll be one massive bang and scraps of Dad splattering all over the street. Farhad tries to pull his jacket round him tighter, but jackets don't work that way. It sort of twists and he lets it drop. I try and straighten his tie and he pulls away.

'You could say no,' I whisper.

'Yeah,' he says. 'Really?'

Dad's next to us. He takes a breath so deep

I hear it over the traffic. I go up and put my arms round him, snuggling my hands underneath his coat like when I was little. Now I'm not far off his height. Farhad stays where he is, half turned away from us with his tie still crooked. Dad unhooks himself from me. We open the door and go in.

So the second time I meet my uncle, he's dead. He's seventeen and he's dead. The boy who did it to him got caught straight away, but that doesn't make it better. You don't stop being dead because some idiot kid from Plaistow gets picked up by the police and held for questioning. You still got a dead boy in a casket. And you want to hear something else stupid? When crap like this happens, you get to know the difference between a coffin and a casket. The coffin's the one shaped like a body, wide, then narrowing down. A casket's shaped like a giant jewellery box, like it's trying to remind you there's something precious in there.

I don't think Jimi-Luke felt precious to no one.

It's weird to think of him and Dad as brothers. Lily, Jimi-Luke's mum, was only fifteen when she had our dad, so Dad grew up with Lily's mum – our G-Gran. Jimi-Luke's from Lily's second load of kids, though Dad said Lily gave up Mum duties on Jimi-Luke just like she did with him. Jimi-Luke lived with his own dad and then with G-Gran, but never seemed to stick. He bounced between his mates' homes and then between inside prison and out and then …

The undertakers are expecting us. They show us through to the chapel of rest. It's a bit like my dentist's waiting room but smaller, with a pair of steel chairs against one wall. In some religions, a mourner stays with the dead person until they're buried. For most of his time here, Jimi-Luke's been alone. Lily's stuck in Jamaica because her new boyfriend can't get a visa to come over. So it's all been down to Dad.

Jimi-Luke's at the end. The room's so small you can't look away. There's a bowl of flowers and a candle next to him which seems wrong for a boy like Jimi-Luke. Dad reckons no one looked at Jimi-Luke with love recently, so before that lid closes down for ever, we're here to show we care. We have to go up to him. We have to look.

Dad goes first and just stands there. I check behind for Farhad. He looks like he's gonna need one of those chairs to collapse on. I think about taking his hand, but I haven't done that for ages. I do it anyway. I reach back and our fingers touch.

I say, 'Together?'

He nods and we move as one to stand beside our dad, to say 'goodbye' to my uncle who never reached eighteen.

*

When we come out the chapel of rest the cars are ready, one for us and one for Jimi-Luke. Both of them have drivers in heavy black suits. Dad used to look like that in his bouncer days. It's such a stupid thought I almost laugh. Dad's paid out for a whole heap of flowers for the top of the casket and a wreath spelling out Jimi-Luke's name. I don't know if the florist charges by letter, but that wasn't gonna be cheap. Dad insisted, though. He said he had to give his brother back his real name because the news made sure they used his street name every time they mentioned what happened.

We follow Jimi-Luke on to the main road. Everyone in Hackney is carrying on their lives as usual, though I know that if the car turned the other way we'd see Jimi-Luke's lamp post. The flowers are mostly dead, but the council haven't moved the pictures of him yet. They're slid into plastic wallets to stop them getting wet and ruined. I like it that someone cares enough to do that.

The others are meeting me at the church. Last time I was here I saw a wedding. I don't know if I'll ever get married. Dad's never going to approve of no one. So far, I've had one boyfriend for two weeks but when he heard who my dad was, he dumped me straight off. To be honest, I don't know if I even want to get married. It doesn't seem to have worked out well for anyone in my family yet.

Sometimes, though, I can't help wondering what it would be like to have all that attention. When you're the big sister and your dad's your mum too, you do a hell of a lot of looking after other people. So imagine that just for a day, everything's for you. Your dress, your hair, your make-up, a limousine like this one. Everyone's waiting for you. The car pulls up, stops and one of the ushers steps forward and opens the door …

Our driver takes us so close he almost drives up the church steps and through the entrance. He gets out and opens the door for us. He does it with respect, like he's genuinely sorry. A couple of police cars are parked up on the side. They say a presence is necessary, just in case. They told Dad they were gonna take away all the bins nearby in case weapons got stored in them. Reprisals, they say. Who the hell's going to reprisal what? Jimi-Luke's already dead.

The car park spaces by the church are all full. People are milling around outside, finishing last-minute cigarettes. I see men in smart suits; women in long weaves and shades; a black bodycon dress; a jumpsuit that looks like it's going out to a rave as soon as the service is done. I don't know if they're from Jimi-Luke's dad's family or the crew Jimi-Luke used to hang with. There's a couple of white women looking nervous. I wonder if they're Jimi-Luke's old teachers, though it's been a long while since he spent time in any school. I don't recognise no one. I feel Dad stretching, making himself taller, his shoulders wider. I look for Sobia, Reba and Kim, but maybe they're already inside.

Then right by the door, Austin slips out from behind a pillar. The boy's so skinny that if he was standing sideways, there'd be no way I could spot him behind there. He's wearing his suit in a different way from how he wears school uniform. He doesn't look like he's trying to fight his way out of it. When I asked him if he'd come, he didn't even look surprised. He said 'yes' straight away. He got it. I almost grin. Austin almost grins back. Luckily Dad doesn't see, as he's striding towards the vicar. She shakes Dad's hand and he follows her inside. Me and Farhad step in behind them and Austin behind me.

Me, Dad and Farhad have to walk up the aisle to the front of the church. When I glance back Austin's sitting in a pew with Reba, Sobia and Kim. That's seven of us: me, Dad, Farhad and the four friends behind me who gave me their afternoon because I asked.

Farhad's fingers are on the squirm again.

All his thoughts must be shunting down into his fingernails looking for a place to get out. Dad's fingers are loose in his lap. He used to do chin-ups on a bar across his bedroom door with Farhad clinging on to his back. I'd be sitting on the floor with his notebook, counting how many he did. I used to think that my dad had the strongest hands in the world. Today they lost their strength.

I go to put my hand on his but then we're told to stand up because they're bringing Jimi-Luke down the aisle.

*

After the service, we drive to the cemetery. Reba can't come because she's meeting the boy who called her a lemming. Kim and Sobia say they've got homework. I don't mind. In the end, out of all the friends I asked, they're the ones who showed. I don't blame Kezia or

Carla or Liv or any of the others. When the police start taking away rubbish bins, you're gonna get worried and it's not like any of them knew Jimi-Luke. I expect Austin to disappear too. I see him chatting to a woman in enormous sunglasses and a black trouser suit. She's standing by a shiny silver car, keys dangling from her hand. She nods and he goes round the other side and gets in her car. We pull into the main road and she indicates and comes up behind us. Ah. They must be coming to the cemetery too. The woman turns on her music. The bass makes the air tremble. Austin's a guitar band boy. He's going to hate it. It's still better than the sound of traffic and Farhad's fingers twisting in and out.

It takes ages to get there. Every water pipe in east London's getting dug up and replaced. When we finally arrive, we still end up crossing over with another funeral that's just ending. There's loads of mourners, mostly white people, though I see an older black woman who reminds me of G-Gran. She's helping a little kid put his coat on and bawling out another one who's kicking gravel at some car tyres.

The undertakers move into place, but this time Dad's there too, his shoulder beneath Jimi-Luke, carrying him up the hill to the grave. The air's cold and damp like touching the inside of a wet plastic bag and the sky out east is getting dark. As we come close I can see the pile of earth and the plastic turf that looks as green as jellybeans. Suddenly, I can't help it. I'm crying. I got my waterproof mascara on and the eyeliner you need acid to burn off, but when I wipe my eyes, my fingers are streaky black. I try to find my breath but it's only working in sobs. I feel a tissue press into my hand. It's Austin. He doesn't say nothing, just walks alongside me, his shiny shoes next to my polite ones and Farhad's good shoes on the other side. I turn to my brother and he's crying too. Austin passes me a tissue for him. I hold Farhad's hand again, but it's like the sun curved away from his fingers long before the rest of London. I try and warm them, but I'm just making him tremble even harder. Then Austin takes my hand. I glance at Dad, but it doesn't matter. Austin's got warmth for all of us.

Thinking

No one stays to see the grave filled, not even Dad. Austin tells me that in Nigeria, funerals are parties. Mourners wear matching clothes in bright colours and they dance and sing and celebrate. Sometimes there's jazz bands and everyone gets food and drink. Once the vicar says the last few words over Jimi-Luke's grave, we're done. It's just our emptiness and the slide of our shoes on the grass.

Dad has to be at work. He says you can't

run five children on a market stall so he's driving as well, doing the overnight shift from eight to six for Suga Cabs.

I say goodbye to Austin. He gives me a tiny smile and watches as I get into the car bringing us back. I should ask Dad if Austin can grab a lift back with us but Dad's in a hurry to go and Farhad looks colder than ghosts.

I glance back and see the gravediggers nearby. Soon all that earth's gonna be sitting on Jimi-Luke's chest with the flowers on top as well. I try and imagine his spirit breaking through like a ninja and bursting out into the cold night. I try to imagine him leaping over the graves, spinning wreaths like nunchucks or swinging from the trees along the main path, like Shia La Beouf in that rubbish *Indiana Jones* film. But I can't imagine it because all I ever seen is Jimi-Luke shouting or dead.

We get home and we all go up to our rooms and change out of our funeral clothes. It looks like Kim tried to rub her make-up out my rug, but she just made it worse. I'm gonna have to get a rug to cover the rug. It's too early for PJs but it's dark outside and the street lights have come on. The one outside my window stays on all night. It bothers Souri, but then she's in the top bunk and gets it full in the eyes and no amount of money is gonna make Ela swap with her.

I hope they're having a good time in Littlehampton, though Ela's already texted me to say it's freezing and everything's closed. She doesn't want to hear why Dad needed her away from here and safe.

I slip into trackies and go downstairs. The chicken curry Dad made yesterday is already heating up and he's boiling the biggest pot of rice. He's probably forgetting that it's just three of us tonight.

Dad says, 'Where's Farhad?'

'In his room. I think he needs some time to himself.'

I bite my lip. I think Dad's going to launch into the usual lecture about how he never got time to himself when he was our age. He had chores to do and God help him if he forgot. He doesn't say it. He lifts the saucepan lid, squints through the steam at the rice and turns off the cooker.

'Are you hungry?'

I'm honest and shake my head. Dad nods. Maybe he can't get it out his head neither – Jimi-Luke in his suit, skin a weird brown-grey, his lips the colour of darkness.

Dad turns the heat off under the curry too. He says, 'Help yourself when you're ready. I'm going up for a bath.'

Maybe he thinks his cab is gonna smell of the graveyard.

As soon as Dad disappears, I text Austin. It's just to say 'thank you'. I wait but he doesn't reply. He's probably gone to prayers.

*

By the time Dad leaves, Farhad still hasn't come out of his room. I hear Dad's voice upstairs calling out instructions, then Dad comes down and gives me the same speech. I've got to double-lock the door, there's no going out, no friends round, no screens after ten. Dad's gonna pass by around midnight to check everything's okay.

I turn on the telly. There's nothing much on. I could watch something on my laptop but our wifi's so crap I spend most of my time watching the buffering. I go upstairs and lie on my bed. It still smells of deodorant and perfume and that spray Reba uses to keep her hair curly. I wonder how she's getting on with the lemming boy. I take out my phone and check her story. She's doing all right, by the looks of it. Kim hasn't posted anything since this morning's picture of the dress she was wearing to the service. I skim through the RIPs, all those strangers going on like they knew Jimi-Luke in real life. But maybe it's better they say something than just ignore it. I'm not sure why I'm feeling so cross. I'm probably missing the little ones. They're a pain when they're here, but there's a big emptiness when they're not.

The sky gets darker and my room gets brighter as the street light blasts through my open curtains. I wonder if Farhad's doing the same thing, just lying there trying to make sense of it. I kind of want to talk about today, but I don't. I'm scared that if I think about it too hard, it will stick to the inside of my head and won't go away. Anyway, he's always better with pictures than words. We've kept a streak going almost three weeks now. He flicks me over a pic and I have to get one back to him in twenty-four hours, then he sends me another one and so on. He usually sends me pictures of trampy-looking buildings or funny cloud shapes. Last night I sent him a picture of the rancid slice of pizza I found under the girls' bunk. I thought it would take his mind off things. I guess not.

I check the time. He's only got an hour or the streak gets broken.

As I'm staring at my screen, I get a notification. It's Farhad. Knowing him, it's gonna be a picture of a curled-up leaf or some flowers or something symbolic. I tap on it, frown and zoom in. It's black shoes hanging over a plank of wood. The hem of some trouser legs, grey material that almost looks black. Smart clothes, that just got worn to a funeral. The plank's high up. I know because I can just about see a rubbish bin on the ground below, a lot of a way below. There's a caption, just one word –

Thinking

Thinking? My brother's thinking of— What the hell, Farhad? What the hell are you thinking? I jump off the bed and run into the boys' room. I don't knock because even if he's doing something he doesn't want me to witness, at least he's there and safe. But he's not there. He's not safe. There's nothing but the boy smell and Darius's made-up bed and Farhad's scuffled one.

I tap his number. Please let him have battery, please let him have battery, please let him have battery. And he does, because he answers.

I don't mean to swear, but I do. Then I say 'sorry'. I listen to his silence for a few seconds then say his name softly, the way I do when he's a bit stressed out and Dad hasn't got time for him.

He says, 'Yeah?'

'Where are you?'

'Thinking.'

'I didn't ask what you're do—' I take a deep breath. 'Where are you thinking, Faz?'

'It doesn't matter.'

'It does to me. I thought you were in your room and you're not. That picture, man. Today was stressful, I know, but—'

The line goes dead. Shit! I try phoning again, but he doesn't answer. I drop my phone on my covers and feel around for my trainers. I remember I crammed everything into the drawer under my bed just before Reba and the squad got here. I pull my trainers out the mess and try and text at the same time.

Please tell me where you are

Silence.

I'm gonna call the police, Faz

He replies straight away.

Do what you want

I text him some more and try and phone, but he doesn't answer. I have to call the police. No choice. But what am I gonna say?

My fourteen-year-old brother's gone out and I don't know where he is.

If the police don't laugh, they'll ask more questions.

How long's he been gone?

Less than an hour.

It's not even eight o'clock. Do you have a special reason for worrying?

Yes. No. I don't know.

Where are your parents?

Mum's in Isfahan and not back any time soon. And Dad, well …

If the police turn up at Suga Cabs asking about Farhad – I rub my eyes – Farhad might as well move to Iran as well.

I squeeze my feet into my trainers. I'm always telling Ela and Souri to undo their laces before taking off their shoes, but I'm a crap role model for that. Sometimes I wonder if I'm a crap role model for everything. I knew – *knew* – that Farhad was struggling today. I didn't do nothing.

Now I gotta do something.

I gotta find him.

I don't even know where to start.

I send out another text, a sort of long, weavy one where I don't know if all the words match with each other. Then I just add one more word at the end.

Help

Austin texts back straight away.

I'm yours

Scaffolding

Sorry, Soraya, I should have sent you a different picture. You understand me too well. You know me like no one else. You know me like Mum should know me and Dad should know me. Man, though. I wish I could laugh right now. Like Dad's ever gonna know me. It sounds harsh, but the more his muscles get bigger, the more his brain gets smaller. It must be rolling round inside his head like a pea in a bucket. Everyone knows that if you take shit like steroids it makes your dick disappear. He says he hasn't popped that stuff for years, but something's wrong, 'cause like every second of every day he's got to prove that he's a man.

You seriously think we got to go easy on him because of Mum? You're his fave, big sis, but even you gotta see it. He's always gotta prove he's a bigger man than anyone else. Than everyone else. It's not my fault he felt small when Mum didn't come back. He doesn't have to make everyone else small too.

I didn't mean to create no drama, but I had to leave the house tonight. You're always kicking off about Souri and Ela, but Darius, man. He takes up all the space. I thought there'd be more room with him away, but I opened the wardrobe and I got hit by his old teddy bear. You know, that demon-looking one with the missing eye and those badges pinned to it. Other days, I would have laughed. Man, laughing's a long way away right now.

You know why Darius doesn't throw nothing away? He says everything's got a memory stuck to it and he don't want to forget nothing.

You remember those old trainers that smelled like a garbage van? You flung them out when he was at football club. You were round Sobia's when the boy came home. He knew straight away because the wardrobe smelled different. He went wild and started yelling. Then Dad went mad because of the noise, so that old woman next door called the police. Once the cops checked we were all right, they were pretty cool about it. One of them was a brother, maybe Dad's age, and he was bigging Dad for raising five kids by himself. The policewoman with him, she didn't look so impressed.

I shoved the teddy back in the wardrobe and I lay down. All I could see was Darius's bed empty. Then his junky Man U duvet faded out and it was chairs and a bowl of flowers and a candle and Jimi-Luke. I pushed my face into the pillow, trying to make inside my head go dark. It didn't work. When you hear that dead people look like they're sleeping, it's bull. Jimi-Luke looked dead. Mouth shut, eyes closed. Boy's dead.

Maybe Darius is right, though. Things got memories caught on them. I got a memory of Jimi-Luke in my pocket. It's slipping through my fingers right now. I can feel every link and the clasp still hooked in. It's making me think some more.

Usually, I do all my thinking on the bus to school. I go upstairs and slide on my headphones. Sometimes, the boys from Pembury get my bus and they're at the back spitting lyrics dragging each other's hair and girl. Their words are fierce and I want to laugh, but I keep my back turned to them and jam up my music, old-time grime from when no one cared if they went mainstream. You don't know, Soraya, but Jimi-Luke introduced me to those tunes, new recs every week.

Every day, I see these new buildings, men up there in their hard hats and hi-vis fixing up scaffolding ready to build taller. It makes me think of Dad, the Big Unfriendly Giant, looking down on people, being in charge. I want that too, but I want to look down on Dad.

You know them snaps I was sending you? The buildings and stuff? Every time I passed them, I was looking and thinking – can I get in there? Can I climb up? In the big sites, there's barriers because the builders know they're getting sued if some kid swings up those poles and crashes down. But then I spotted an old house on the main route. I sent you that one too. It looks like it's haunted, sis, a proper Monster House with scaffolding all round it like a cage. So many poles, it's like the man in charge got the order wrong and added too many zeros. Every time I passed by, I saw more places to slot in my hands and my feet. The house was empty too, so no one would catch me climbing past their windows.

That was my plan, Soraya. I was gonna climb up to the highest platform, up past the roof and no one was gonna see me unless I wanted them to.

My plan got interrupted because I saw God.

Mates

Me and Austin meet up in McDonald's. I've never done a proper meet-up with a boy, the sort of thing Reba does. She spends hours getting ready beforehand and posts pictures of her outfits and lipstick and asks our opinion. Then when she's with the boy she takes sneaky pics and sends them direct. One day she's gonna go public by mistake and get cussed out for it.

Austin's only ever seen me in school

uniform and then in my funeral dress and now like this. If I post a picture of me now, Reba's gonna need a helicopter to pick her up quick and drop her off at A & E. My trainers are all beaten down at the back and I'm still wearing my washed-out Primark trackies with a coat over the top. I had to borrow Souri's Youth Games cap because my hair looks like someone's trying to weave baskets with it. Even if the apocalypse drops right now and balls of fire start falling from the sky, there's no way I'm taking off that hat. I've probably got blots of make-up all over my face because I forgot to do a wipe-off after the funeral.

Austin's sitting right at the back. I work my way past every single table before I get to him. It's cold outside but it's warm in here and I can feel my hair soaking up the sweat beneath Youth Games as I try not to fall over the

Peacocks bags and the buggies and roadmen with their legs all spread out taking up half the floor. I sit down opposite him. We've never really been alone together before. We talk, we talk all the time, but it's school talk where you're throwing jokes at each other across the classroom. And man, Austin can throw! For a short boy, he's got one big mouth on him.

He says, 'Are you okay?'

I nod, then I shake my head.

He pushes a cup towards me. 'I got you a hot chocolate. It's not proper, though. It's chocolate syrup and hot water.'

I give him a sideways look. 'Do you check out everything you eat?'

He grins. 'My sister Binrin's doing a non-dairy thing. She's been through the whole menu reading the ingredients.'

'And?'

'She says a Big Mac's cool. No cheese. Light on the sauce.'

'Big Macs come halal?'

He shrugged. 'That doesn't bother her. Soon as Dad went back to Nigeria, Binrin stopped being Muslim. She doesn't do any religions but she's had to promise Mum she won't tell any of the aunties that. Mum's always been Christian. It's just me who's Muslim now. Families aren't easy.'

Yeah, that's why we're here. 'I have to find Farhad,' I say. 'I just don't know where to start.'

Austin reaches into his rucksack and pulls out a notebook and a pencil.

He says, 'Let's see the photo. Maybe there's some clues.'

I shake my head. 'We sent snaps. They're gone. I should have screengrabbed it. And I should have shut up and just let him talk.'

Austin touches my hand. 'It's okay, Soraya. We'll find him. Who's his friends?'

'He hasn't really got any. He had a couple of good mates in our first primary school but we moved when he was in Year Three.' I almost tell him how Dad didn't like the way people talked about us and thought all the teachers were looking down on him. 'Farhad's always been quiet. He doesn't make friends easy.'

'I've seen him with a crowd at school.'

'They're not really his friends. He kind of hangs around with them, but Dad doesn't like us going to other people's houses.'

Or other people coming to ours. Today was exceptional circumstances.

Austin's pencil's hanging, waiting for its job. 'What about cousins or anyone like that?'

'Mum's got a sister, but she's not in London. All her kids go to private school. They don't have anything to do with us. There's a sister between Dad and Jimi-Luke, but she got married and moved to Germany.' I have a think. 'There was G-Gran, but she died five years ago.'

'G-Gran? Like gravitational force grandma?'

In spite of myself, I laugh. 'She was my great-grandma. Dad lived with her when he was little.'

Austin's mouth opens and closes again.

I say, 'You were you going to ask why, weren't you?'

He looks a bit embarrassed.

I say, 'It's okay. I don't really know the details, but Dad doesn't have much to do with his mum. He doesn't even call her 'Mum'. She's Lily. He had to phone her about

Jimi-Luke's funeral, but they just ended up shouting at each other. Lily's in Jamaica, but I could still hear her in our sitting room. Farhad loved G-Gran, though. He was always round there.'

'Where did she live?'

'Near Old Street.'

Austin writes it down. 'Any other places or things he does?'

I think hard. 'G-Gran used to take him to the cinema.' Just him. Never me. I used to be vexed as hell thinking he was getting special treats. She must have seen he needed it the most.

'So he could have gone to see a film.'

'He took the picture outside. He was high up, like on a platform.'

I can almost see the thoughts rippling across Austin's face. I don't want to say anything in case I disturb them. Finally, he points to something behind me.

'Like that?'

I turn round and frown. 'The door?'

'Across the road.'

An old pub's been knocked down and they're putting up posh new flats. The building's halfway done and covered in scaffolding.

I say, 'Yes. Like that.'

Farhad?

Mum used to say my brother's name like a sigh. I wish it really was a sigh, so it could waft out the Maccy D's air vent and gust round London until it finds him. I want him to understand that if he's thinking something really bad, I've got his back.

Austin says, 'Do you want to call the police?'

'Not yet. It's only been an hour or so.'

'He did seem pretty shook up at the funeral …'

'Dad made us go to the chapel of rest to say goodbye properly.'

'Open casket?'

'Yes.'

'Damn! That's definitely gonna shake you up if you're not ready for it. So I presume you're not calling your dad, neither?'

'You've seen my dad.'

Austin nods slowly. 'Yeah. He's the guy who looks like he can carry the world on his shoulders and most of Saturn too. But that doesn't mean he doesn't care.'

He cares too much.

I say, 'Him and Farhad don't get on that well. They're different. It's hard to explain.'

Austin looks serious. 'No. I get it. Having a dad on a different continent really has its advantages. I just need to check something.'

I watch him studying his phone. His hair's cut short, which always makes me smile. His best mate, Bailey, has this ginger afro. It's so big it makes the air glow around him like he's an angel.

Austin says, 'Do you know what time Farhad left home?'

'It must have been when I was upstairs. Around half seven, or just before.'

'Did he take his travelcard?'

I should have checked! I should have damn well checked. I almost tripped over his schoolbag on the way out. Farhad keeps it in there now because Dad went off on one last time it dropped out of Farhad's pocket and never got found.

I say, 'I don't know.'

Austin slaps his forehead. 'It was a dumbass

question. Why should you know?' He fiddles with his phone again. 'I know it sounds weird, but has he ever talked about buildings and stuff?'

'It's not weird,' I say. 'He sends me snaps of them. I never asked him why. I thought it was just to keep our streak going.'

'Can you remember any of them?'

I think hard, but it's like my brain's crying because all my thoughts are blurry. I realise I'm crying for real again. Austin hands me a tissue. He must have packets of them Sellotaped in a row up his sleeve because he produces them pretty quick.

He says, 'Are you sure you don't want to tell your dad?'

I want to say 'no, I'm not sure' and call Dad right away. But there's no way. We can't go back to the way things were after Mum left.

I can feel all the tears backing up behind my eyelids. I take a deep breath.

'Dad's coming to check on us at midnight. We have to find Farhad before then.'

Missing

Austin's got a rucksack like Mary Poppins's bag. So far he's pulled out a flask with an extra mug, some chocolate biscuits and some ginger ones in case I don't like chocolate, an A4 notebook and a pencil and a portable phone charger. He's looked up all the bus stops between my house and Farhad's school and we're walking slowly, checking down side streets and looping back on to the main road. It's taking time and it's getting colder. I know our family don't believe in any gods, but I'm praying like my face is gonna burst that Dad doesn't hit a quiet spot and pass by home early. He hasn't yet or he'd be hammering his 'call Soraya' button like Thor beating up on Hulk.

I check my phone again. No message from Dad. None from Farhad, neither.

I say, 'We need to turn off here. Suga Cabs' office is opposite the station and just my luck, Dad'll be parked outside having a coffee.'

'Sure.'

I feel the silence before Austin's next question. Then he comes out with it.

'Why does your dad act all scary like that?'

'It's like you said. He cares about us.'

Austin takes a step away from me. I realise I've bounced my answer back too hard. I breathe out and my crossness seems to steam out my nose and shine in the cold. I can see the railway bridge ahead. We turn off into a side road.

I say, 'Our mum left us when I was in Year Four. Her dad was ill and she went back to Iran to look after him. She wanted to take us, but Dad said Iran was too dangerous. I've looked it up since and there was about three different wars going on, so he was right. None of us believed him at the time, though. I just wanted my mum.'

Talking about her feels like Thor's swapped Hulk for my heart. It's under my ribs being squashed flat.

Austin says, 'Do you hear from her?'

'She used to phone us.'

'Used to?'

'Yeah.'

After she stopped phoning, I'd creep into the boys' room and me and Farhad would write letters to her begging her to come back. Farhad made me ask Dad for her address because he reckoned Dad liked me the most and wouldn't shout too much. He didn't shout. He just gave me this really hurt look and said nothing. I think Farhad's still got our letters in an old trainer box in the wardrobe.

I carry on talking, trying to make my words slower than my steps. 'I don't know why Mum stopped phoning us. Maybe Dad told her not to call any more.'

I wait for Austin to have an opinion. People always do, angry for Dad or for Mum, because one of them has to be right or wrong. We walk on some more. We'll have to turn back on to the main road soon.

He says, 'Do you miss her?'

'I don't know.' It's the first time I've said

that. I always say yes. It's easier. 'I think I should, because she's my mum. Or maybe all the things that happened next won't let me think about her properly.'

What happened next? His eyes say it. His words don't have to.

I tell him. 'Dad's always had a reputation. He's always had a temper. When I was little, he went to prison because a car nearly knocked him off his bike. Dad swore it was deliberate. He knew who did it and he went to their house and punched them.'

We turn right, back to Farhad's bus route.

'After Mum went, there was all these rumours that Dad had done something to her. We'd go to school and everyone would turn around and look at us. There was this teaching assistant who wouldn't let it go. As soon as the teacher turned his back, she'd be asking.

'Did your dad ever hit your mum? That's why she's gone, isn't it?' Farhad got into a fight with this idiot called Brent who kept dissing Dad, and, well, Farhad's not a fighter. He came out worse. All of us had to go and see the welfare officer. She'd heard that Dad hit us too. Dad was even getting it tough at work. He was a warehouseman in Tesco and none of the other workers would talk to him.'

Austin says, 'That's rough, man.'

'It was. Because Dad never hit any of us, though I think he sometimes came close. One day, Dad came back from work with loads and loads of shopping. He said none of us needed to go to school no more. We didn't need to leave the flat at all, because people outside didn't understand and he was the only one who could look after us properly.'

Austin says, 'How long were you off school?'

'Less than two weeks. It was sort of fun. We put on our school uniforms and pretended we were soldiers.' I smile, remembering it. 'We'd go sliding across the sitting-room floor on our bellies, hiding from the enemy. Then the school sent the police round and they threatened to break in. We had to talk to social workers but maybe that wasn't too bad, because they helped us move away and start new schools. Dad had to see a counsellor. That was part of the deal and I think it helped him too.'

We walk along for a few minutes. The ends of my fingers are tingling with cold.

I say, 'Do you miss *your* dad?'

Austin shakes his head. 'Not really, though it was strange when he left. He's a bit older than Mum and he was never happy in England. He got married again when he went back and now he's got the family he always wanted.'

'What do you mean?'

'He just seems happier.'

Austin doesn't say anything for a while. I'm trying to work out if I should say something else, but then he moves closer until our shoulders are touching.

He says, 'What if you've got a friend who really wants to help you? If your dad found out, on a scale from Ant Man to Hulk, how much damage would he do?'

I nudge his shoulder with mine. 'I'm gonna put you two in a room together and lock the door so you can find out.'

'I'm asking for a friend, remember?' He grins.

'Just make sure you got a dustpan and brush to clean up what's left of them.'

He stops walking. I almost smack into him.

'Look!'

I look. It's a house covered in so much scaffolding it uses up half the road. There's boards around the entrance, but I reckon you can easily get through from the neighbour's garden.

Austin raises an eyebrow. 'What do you think?'

I rummage round in my head, trying to remember the snaps Farhad sent me. But I shouldn't have to do that. If Farhad's here, I should know. We used to have a connection, but it's like the cold's made it freeze and break.

I say, 'Yeah, it looks familiar.'

God

So this is where I got to, Soraya, higher than Dad and just below God.

Not a proper god, just in case you think I've gone full headcase. I saw an Asgard god. Guess which one? Yeah, there's only one, right? I saw Heimdall, all-seeing, all-hearing guardian of the Bifrost. Except this time he's wearing a purple jumper and advertising cable TV.

You got it, sis? I'm with Idris Elba. The god

in the Sky ads. His face is big enough to fit on the side of a bus. Idris, the man I wish I could be, is pasted right next to me.

Feels like a Frost Giant's been up here first, though. The cold's so sharp I can't move my toes, but at least it stops me feeling the squeeze from these old man's shoes. They're last year's. Last year's, man! Dad wasn't ready to hear nothing about how my feet had grown since he bought them. But then he's never ready to hear nothing from me any time. Up here it doesn't matter. I can shout until I bust my throat and no one's gonna hear. I can't fight the buses or the sirens or the music. That means I don't have to bother trying.

I should have grabbed my trainers, though. And some gloves. Me and Darius got a whole drawer of those magic ones that start small and stretch over any size hand. Dad got them from the women in the next stall to him. Bet you and Souri and Ela have got a load too. Darius reckons the glove woman wants to start something with Dad. I want to turn up outside her stall and yell, 'Don't! He ain't worth it!'

Damn. My ears are freezing up. If they touch these poles, I'm gonna be stuck here 'til summer.

Idris was watching me when I took that snap for you, sis. Afterwards, I stood up with my toes sticking out over the planks looking at the tower block on the other side of the railway track. It made me think about G-Gran's place. I know you all got jealous because she gave me more time than you. But I hope you understand now. I needed something for myself. Our flat's always full. When Mum left, there should have been more room, but it was worse. Dad got bigger and so did Mum. She was only in my head but she filled me all up. The counsellor told Dad I should have my own space. Dad laughed out loud when he told me. He said you can't just buy extra space in Tesco. But what I got was an extra person. I got G-Gran.

It's where I met Jimi-Luke. I knew about him. He's not a secret and once Dad showed me some baby pics of him. Sometimes Jimi-Luke was at his dad's in Leyton. Sometimes he'd be putting on his pyjamas and brushing his teeth next to me at G-Gran's. Later I found out that when Jimi-Luke was little, Dad wanted him to live with us. It was when Mum was pregnant with the twins, so pretty crap timing. I was only four but I still remember them yelling. Man! We were living in the eastest part of Hackney, but there must have been folks living in the southest part of Croydon that heard Mum and Dad when they got going.

I don't know how many floors the block opposite's got because I can't see the bottom to count. G-Gran was the queen of the twenty-first floor. Sometimes she'd take me and Jimi-Luke on to the balcony. Our favourite time was when it was getting dark and the lights were coming on and we could see people through their windows before they shut their curtains. G-Gran would make up stories about them. That woman there was Goldilocks, all grown up, making dinner for the three bears who took a human shape for just one hour every day so they could sit down and eat together. And, see there? That's the phone box where Superman changed when he came on holiday to London and needed to beat up a few badman. G-Gran said

London was ours. We owned London. But I
don't own nothing.

Funny thing is, G-Gran's block held so
many people, but the noise got quieter the
higher you went up. Jimi-Luke laughed at me.
He said I'd never heard quiet, not proper
quiet. On G-Gran's balcony, we could see
parks and trees, but Jimi-Luke had lived
further away than that. One time, he was in a
children's home in the countryside. He tried
to draw it for me. It came out like the
houses I drew when I was six. It had a door in
the middle and windows either side. There
was a long drive with trees and bright green
grass and a vegetable garden. He said that
after the sun went down, the sky was so dark
he could see every single star. He drew Mars
for me in red and coloured everything round
it black. He said it was like he could reach

into the sky and pull it out.

The sky in London looks like God spilled tea across it. Not you, Idris. You're a man who keeps hold of his drinks. I mean proper God, if there is one. Right now, I'm looking up at the big brown stain with some skinny clouds thrown at it, like proper God got scared his mum's gonna find out and had an accident so he's splashed some bleach around to hide it.

I can't see no stars at all, just lights from the planes. When G-Gran died, I used to look for her up there, because that's where Dad said she was. I tried to work out which star was hers, even though I could hardly see none and I didn't even believe it was true. I want it to be true tonight. I hope Jimi-Luke and G-Gran find each other in the darkness.

It was cold up by the graveyard, but I thought that's just because it's a graveyard.

There aren't never gonna be no loungers or barbecues there. Man, though, it's way colder up here. I feel like Anna when she got turned to ice by Elsa. And yeah, Soraya, I'm never gonna forgive you for making me know every song in *Frozen*.

I wish I'd worn a T-shirt under my shirt, but then the jacket wouldn't have fit. Do you remember that old woman who used to live above us in Hind House? She died, man, because she didn't want to put on no heating. I was glad when they moved us out because I hated passing her door. I used to think her ghost was sitting just behind it waiting for me. She was going to burst out and pull me in. Her fingers were gonna be like icicles, sharp and shiny and they'd poke into my ears and probe through my brain and I'd go cold and die.

Damn! I just shivered so hard, I almost fell off the platform. Maybe the old woman's ghost is really sitting next to me now. Maybe her fingers are already stretching out.

Thing is, Soraya, if she kills me, I deserve it.

Connection

Austin's ahead of me, making like he's Tom Cruise in *Mission Impossible*. Except we're not climbing the outside of a skyscraper. We're creeping through the neighbour's bushes towards the scaffolding. I try not to make no noise, but it's hard when you got a thorn spiking through your coat into your arm. One just scraped my face. The people in this house are going to open their door tomorrow morning and find my skin hanging from their holly bush. An ambulance just screamed by. I hope it passes back this way to sew me together again.

A couple of police cars shoot by. Me and Austin freeze, though half of Austin's rucksack is sticking out the bush. If anyone looks, they can't miss us. No one does look, though. Austin says there's important football on telly tonight. I don't know about that. My family don't follow God nor football. Austin's family worships two gods plus five football teams if you count England and Nigeria. He told me earlier that he's even named after a Super Eagle. I didn't know there were any birds called Austin. When he finished laughing, he told me his mum called him after a Nigerian footballer.

The police cars disappear. We push our way through the rest of the bush. The wall behind it is low enough for me to climb over without embarrassing myself. The last thing I need is Austin yanking me over from the other side.

We stand at the bottom of the scaffolding, brushing twigs off us, and look up at the crisscross poles.

I say, 'On a scale from Ant Man to Hulk, how small d'you have to be to fit through those gaps?'

Austin makes a face. 'If you're all Hulk like me, you're gonna have a problem.'

I smile for him, touch some poles and look up again.

'I don't think Farhad's here,' I say, 'It doesn't feel like the right place and I didn't see all that scaffolding in the picture he sent me.'

Austin raises an eyebrow. 'I left my forehead in that bush and you're telling me that now?'

He sees my face.

'Sorry,' he says. 'Bailey's always telling me I have to learn to keep my mouth shut, because one day some one's gonna put a fist in it. You really think this isn't the place?'

I want to explain about me and Farhad's connection. It's not a proper one like the twins reckon they've got. If me and Farhad got put in a science lab and tested, we would probably come out as nothing. But there is something, probably from all the time we hung out together after Mum left.

Instead I say, 'In the picture, there was a rubbish bin and no poles. The nearest bin's probably back by the station. And Farhad was standing up. He couldn't stand up here – there'd be loads of poles in the way.'

My phone goes off. Farhad loaded up Lady Leshurr's 'Queen's Speech' as my ringtone and the words are coming out loud and clear. I grab for it and we both drop down crouching, listening to see if the neighbour's door opens.

'Answer it!' Austin whispers.

I check it. My stomach almost lands on Austin's feet. 'It's Dad!'

Lady Leshurr carries on for a few more seconds until Dad rings off. Then the phone buzzes up a message. All huddled up in the leaves and the dirt and the rubbish, I want to start crying again.

I say, 'If Farhad was here, he would have come down when he heard that. He'd have known it was me.'

I wipe my face. Austin opens his rucksack and takes out the Thermos flask. He pours out some tea and hands it to me. The steam's so hot it makes my face tingle and the tea tastes like he's strained it through a bag of sugar. I drink half and pass the cup back to him. He finishes it, screws the cup on to the flask and replaces it in his rucksack.

He says, 'Ready?'

I nod.

We push our way back through the bush. It's easier now because we've already made a gap. We check the street's empty then walk down the path in front of the neighbour's house like we live there. Someone must have scored a goal because everyone in the house suddenly cheers and I jump. We cross the street and I stare up at the scaffolding. No, Farhad's definitely not there.

Austin says, 'Are you going to call your dad back?'

I want to look at my phone and not look at the same time. Sometimes, I get a weird pulling feeling at the side of my eyes when I know I'm gonna have to deal with something bad. Right now, it feels like my eyes are being stretched round to the back of my head. I make myself check. Dad's left a voice message and a text. He's on the way to Heathrow. I show the text to Austin.

He says, 'Your dad's gonna be back at eleven-thirty?' He laughed. 'He better have an alien in a basket on his roof.' He raises an eyebrow. 'You know, like *E.T*? And the flying bikes?'

'Yes. I know.'

'Because it's nearly ten now.'

'I know that too! Maybe your mate Bailey's right. You don't always have to say something.'

Austin opens his rucksack and fishes out a chocolate energy bar. He offers it to me. 'I know. Sorry.'

So am I.

I take the bar and try to smile. 'What else have you got in your bag?'

'It was getting cold when I left. I brought a spare jumper and a scarf for Farhad.'

Man.

I say, 'I didn't mean to shout at you. I just don't know what to do.'

Austin reaches across and squeezes my fingers. 'Call your dad, Soraya. You can't deal with all this by yourself.'

I say, 'But I'm not alone, am I?'

Austin grins. 'True. You do have the wonder that's me.' His smile drops. 'But your dad really needs to know about this.'

My phone's in my hand. I tap 'return call'. Dad picks up straight away.

Snap

I want to call you, Soraya, but my battery's dead. I used the last power to check what happens when a person gets too cold. First, you're gonna get slurred speech. I'm only talking in my head, but I sound all right to me. Next, you're gonna feel tiredness. When we walked out the chapel of rest, I thought I was never gonna sleep again, because every time I closed my eyes, I'd see Jimi-Luke. Not the body in the coffin, but the real one with his eyeballs always looking like they were going to bounce out his sockets and his mouth too small for all those teeth.

Did you see how vexed Dad got when the news kept calling up his street name? Jimi-Luke Alleyne, also known as Grillz. You imagine all these stupid people looking it up and finding a picture of a rapper or something, with his lips all pulled back like a mad dog, flashing a mouth full of gold and jewels. And for them people, that's gonna say everything they need to know about Jimi-Luke.

Jimi-Luke didn't have no metal in his mouth apart from the filling he showed me when he came back from the dentist that time. His mouth had hung on to some milk teeth when his permanent ones came through. Jimi-Luke wasn't Grillz. He was *Bare* Grillz. It was jokes. He had too many teeth. That's what made him look so wrong in the chapel of rest. When he was alive, his mouth never stayed shut.

I think I'm feeling the tiredness, Soraya. Even though Jimi-Luke's still on my mind, my eyes keep closing. It's like the cold's got a lasso and it's pulled me down flat. These planks are filthy, man, but I have to rest up a bit. The back of my head's gonna have a workman's footprint stamped on it in dust. If Dad was here, he'd be roaring about my suit getting mash up, but my body don't want to stay upright. And Dad isn't here.

I'm looking straight into God's eyes. That's Heimdall god, not proper God. Heimdall, you don't look so good close up, not like when I see you from the ground. The paper round your chin's all flapping. You need some Palmer's. It's fast-absorbing, no greasy feel, so your hands won't be slipping all over the Bifrost controls. And no, man, I don't go round remembering all the words on the labels. But my little bruv, Darius, does. It irritates the hell out of me. He always reads the back of bottles. Every single little detail. Every medicine, every lotion.

How am I looking from up there, Heimdall? I think my bones are crumbling and ready to break off like those icebergs you see on TV. You and me. One more gust of wind and we're going to float away together.

I should keep my hands in my pockets, but then I got to touch it. Though my fingers are so cold, I won't feel nothing soon.

Did you see Jimi-Luke's hands, Soraya? They cleaned up his fingernails. He'd got the same suit as me. Did you know Dad bought two of them? I did work experience in mine, Jimi-Luke went to court in his.

Jimi-Luke came round that last time wanting help. Me and Darius, we had our bedroom window open and heard him and Dad yelling at each other by the front door. Dad said he'd been pushed too far and he had to use his energy to take care of his real family. Us, Soraya. We were his real family and Jimi-Luke got excluded. He said Jimi-Luke had run out of opportunities and had to get himself out of his stupidass situation on his own. He said Jimi-Luke didn't care about no one else but himself, and if he wanted to hang round the street until some little boy with a grudge and a gun shot him up, that was his business. Not Dad's business. Not the family business. Jimi-Luke's business.

I should have come out my room and told Dad. Jimi-Luke *did* care. He helped me. It was our business.

I wish I'd brought my coat, Soraya. This wind feels like it's got nails in it. And Heimdall, man, it's blowing so hard it's making your face ruffle. Or do you want to say something to me? Your mouth's still pasted shut, but you don't have to talk. Do your telepathy thing. Zap your words straight into my head.

I'm waiting ... Okay, Heimdall, I can't hear nothing. But maybe that's the next sign of too much cold. Confusion. Of course I'm confused. I'm having a conversation with a Norse god who looks like a brother.

And I'm confused that my uncle is dead. It should be the other way round. I want to stand up and shout – 'It's me! I should be the one in the graveyard!'

I can't stand up, though. Too much tiredness.

Soraya, if you were here, you'd tell me to

calm down on the drama. Sit up, slide down one of them poles and come home. But I'm not done with thinking yet.

I told Jimi-Luke about Armand and his crew. I didn't mean to. No. I have to be truthful. I *did* mean to. I told him because I had no one else to tell. Soraya, you kind of knew some things, but not everything. You didn't know that Armand was the son of the wasteman Dad punched out that time after he nearly knocked Dad off his bike. You didn't know that every time one of them pushed me, or tripped me, or threatened nastiness to you and Souri and Ela, it was Dad they wanted. You didn't know that they made their plans to rush Dad's stall and mash up all his goods. They wanted to prod Dad until he roared and then they were going to come for him.

I didn't tell Jimi-Luke straight away. You

know how Dad always goes on that he can handle himself. He doesn't need no help from no one. And then ... and then I thought that if Dad wasn't here – not dead, Soraya, but inside again – we'd be better. When I'm around him I feel like my stomach's full of dust.

So I left it. Until last month. It was that time you sent me round the corner to get bread and teabags. I took the short cut through the square next to the flats. If I hadn't had my music on, I would have heard them. There was just three of them, filling the place with their noise. It was Armand, another boy I seen before and a girl in Pitt Academy uniform, cotching out by the benches. They saw me first. The boys were quick. They got me before I could run. The girl just sat on the bench watching like we were gonna act out *Cinderella* for her. I nearly laughed, Soraya.

These were the two ugliest sisters anyone was ever going to have.

Even when they were pulling at me and shouting, I knew it was all front. People were passing through the square, on their phones, looking ahead, but still checking out the situation. Someone was going to call the police if they saw blood.

The boy held my arms behind my back while Armand threw the insults. He knew about when Dad went weird. He started on Mum, shouting off his dirty mouth about where she was and how many men she's doing it with. He's telling me how good Souri's gonna look in a year's time. I'm burning up so much I think all of us are going to take off like a rocket. Then Armand sees my chain. Mum's chain. You know how I usually make sure it's under my clothes, but it must have slid out when I was lacing up my trainers. Armand's hand's on my neck. I hear the snap. I see gold slide through his fingers down on to the dirt. He picks it up and I try and grab it back, but he pushes me down. Then him and the boy and the girl walk away.

You understood, Soraya. Any time I wore that chain, I knew it had touched Mum's skin. It made her close. I was there on the ground in the plastic bags and beer cans, and I touch my neck to see if she's still there. It was like trying to touch a shadow when the sun's going in.

When I got home, you bawled me out for taking so long. I didn't tell you. I couldn't. I knew you would go out looking for them and I was scared. I told Jimi-Luke instead. I told him because I knew what he would do and he did it. He called his big cousin. They came down to our estate and searched out Armand. They found him chilling out on the same bench I told them about. I should have described Armand better, though everyone says him and his little brother look like twins. Same eyes, same hair, same bad mouth. Jimi-Luke saw the gold round the boy's neck and he snatched back what he thought was mine.

Family business.

Jimi-Luke called me and I collected it from him. I didn't tell him it was wrong. The wrong chain. The wrong brother. Not with his big cousin screwfacing next to him. I know what it's like to be small and I didn't want to do that to Jimi-Luke.

The chain I got in my pocket is wider than Mum's. It's stronger. The snap would have been louder. The broken link could have been fixed. Dad's got pliers, but I was never going to wear it. I wanted to give it back to Jimi-Luke today, slip it in his jacket pocket or rest it on his chest. He died for it. But then I'd be burying him with a curse. So, it's still here, in *my* pocket.

You see the police today, Soraya? They were waiting for Armand's little brother to show and cause stress. But I reckon his little brother's at home wondering how long Armand's gonna be locked up. Wondering if Armand's ever gonna be safe again. Dad says he's seen so many boys like Armand, a big man on the prison landing and in the canteen. But it's different when you're all alone in your cell with just you and the walls and the bunk.

Maybe Armand's gonna see more than the walls. Maybe he'll see Jimi-Luke sitting on the bunk next to him, because I feel like Jimi-Luke's here now. He's making the cold colder and the dark darker. If I open my eyes, he might disappear, but I can't. My eyes are shut. My mouth is shut. When I breathe in, the night smells of earth and flowers and candles.

I'm trying to move my fingers but they're stuck. I want to feel the chain, each link, one at a time, pressing into my skin. There's thirty-two links. I counted them.

Heimdall, use your god-power and help me touch it. Help me turn my head and open my eyes.

Yeah, thank you, brother. That's better.

The street light makes the chain trickle orange and yellow. One, two, three – the links flicker and fall.

I see my breath in the glow.

I see Jimi-Luke in his suit sitting next to me. He's reaching out his hand.

You died for it. It's yours. I let the chain fall.

Links

Dad's on his way. He's over by Hammersmith but he says the traffic's moving quick. He's gonna meet me at home and then we'll plan what to do next. He didn't roar. He just said 'okay'. That was it.

I think about how hard today must have been for him. He buried his little brother and now his son's out there in the cold in just his suit and shirt and whatever's in his head that made him run like that. Farhad, up there …

I try his phone again, but it goes straight to messages.

Austin could have got his bus home, but he's still with me. I know he's got to say his last prayers before midnight, but he says he's got time. He's given me some spare gloves he had in his rucksack. One minute we're by houses, the next we're passing bars and restaurants. They're busy. A girl in hot pants and knee boots staggers out one of the new places with a drink in her hand.

I say, 'She looks like Wonder Woman.'

Austin nods. 'It's definite. You're Marvel.'

'Or what?'

'DC.'

'I'm both, I suppose. Me and Farhad watch all the films with the little ones.' Three of us on the sofa, two of us on cushions on the floor. Dad bought us a popcorn machine from the market so we're all munching away so loud it's sometimes hard to hear the film.

Me and Austin walk on some more.

'He'll be all right,' Austin says.

I want that to be true. I want to get home and hear Farhad blasting Kano from his bedroom. But all I keep seeing is my brother in the casket instead of Jimi-Luke. Both of them were wearing the same suits. I'd forgotten how Dad bought two, one for work experience and one for court.

Jimi-Luke was in court again two weeks ago. He was accused of assault. Armand was waiting when he came out. He had a knife and he used it.

Me and Austin carry on, past the smoke and music and laughing until we're on the quieter roads. Austin's hand's been swinging closer and closer until our gloves are almost making static. Our hands stop, palm to palm. Austin's fingers tighten round mine. We carry on walking.

He says, 'Will your dad go mad if he sees us together?'

'Maybe.' *Yes. He'll want to kill you.*

'I don't want to make things worse, but I can stay with you until he gets back.'

I shake my head. 'You've made things better. Masses better. But Dad's really stressed and I don't want him having a go.'

'You said he was all right on the phone.'

'He sounded like he couldn't roar no more, even if he wanted to. It doesn't mean it's gone for good.'

Austin leans forward and I think he's going to try and kiss me, but he picks a twig out my hair. Then another one. I brush a cobweb from his eyebrow.

I say, 'I better go.'

'I'll walk you to your block.'

'You don't have to.'

'I want to.'

We don't move.

He says, 'Look, Soraya, I know you're probably holding out for Idris Elba, but if you—'

'Who?'

He doesn't get my joke. He points across the road. 'You know! Him!'

There's an old Sky TV poster pasted across a hoarding on a busted old pub. The sign says that it's gonna change into a noodle bar once the refurbishment's done. Idris is holding his arms wide like he's trying to measure how much we should want cable.

I want to say, 'I know who Idris is.' I want to say, 'It's not him I want right now.' And I could have said it. But it's like Idris has reached out from his poster, linked his fingers behind my back and is pulling me towards him.

Austin follows me across the road. He says in a small voice, 'I was just joking about the brother, there. I know all girls are gonna make him number one. But I don't mind being second choice.'

I put my finger on Austin's lips and squint up at the poles and platforms. He looks confused. I stay there listening, but all I can hear is the helicopter over another part of Hackney. I move closer and touch the metal pole in front of me. That's when I see it, a sliver of gold snaking through the cracks in the planks above me. I hold out my hand and it lands in my palm. It's chunky, rich man's gold. It's snapped, though the clasp is still done up. I take off my glove and squeeze it. It feels cool and hot at the same time. I imagine it being torn from a neck and thrown out into the cold air.

I move back on to the pavement again.

Farhad? Was it you pulling me here?

I catch Idris's eye but he's not giving away nothing. The chain's in the palm of my hand and I'm rubbing it like I'm expecting a genie to pop up and answer my questions. That's when Austin shoves me hard in the back. I turn round to cuss him, but he's not there. He's round the side, getting a better look up the scaffolding. I sniff. I smell earth and flowers and candles. A burst of it, like when you open a packet of flour too quickly and some puffs out.

I put a hand out to steady myself.

'Are you okay?' Austin runs over to me.

'You didn't push me, right?'

He gives me a confused look. 'Man, my arms aren't that long.'

Thor's working away at my heart again. Bang, slam. Bang, slam. Bang, slam.

I say, 'Can you smell something?'

Austin grabs my arm. 'You've had a long day, Soraya. I'll take you home and I'll stay with you until your dad comes. I don't care if he bawls me out.'

I shake him off. The smell's gone now, if it was ever there. But something else is there. At least, I think so. Like a chain, but thicker, with fat, silver links that look like they're made from light and air.

I yell, 'Farhad!'

Nothing.

Austin says, 'You think he's here?'

'I know he is.' I point to a rubbish bin. 'That's the one in the photo.'

Austin nods. 'Okay. Do you want me to go first?'

I should say 'no', leap on to it and swing up. But my body's not made for acrobatics. Austin climbs on to the bin, reaches up and grabs the edge of the lowest platform, heaving himself on.

He calls down, 'There's a ladder at the end so we can get up to the next level.'

It takes me two goes to get onto the bin. Even if it took me a hundred, I was going to do it. Austin reaches out and helps me on to the platform next to him.

I say, 'You're still wearing your rucksack.'

He nods. 'Spare jumper and scarf, remember?'

I kiss him on his forehead. He looks

shocked, but I don't have time for nothing else. I cup my mouth and shout. 'Farhad!'

I don't know if Farhad hears me, but those links look almost solid, coiling down from the top of this building, straight through all the platforms, then wrapping around me. It's pulling me past Austin towards the ladder.

I take Austin's hand as I sweep past him.

'Farhad!'

It's both of us yelling this time. And just for a second, there's no helicopters or sirens or music. I hear my name. Soraya sounds like a sigh too. Mum never told me that. The links are tugging at me, but I don't let go of Austin. This chain's strong. It can hold me and Austin, Farhad and even Dad too. It'll loop round Darius and Ela and Souri and maybe, maybe it's long enough to reach Mum. Even if it does, it will never break.

I look up. There's wood and metal and Idris. There's London's blue-brown sky and planes like slow-motion stars. There's shadows like hands, a face, a body and a chain that's shimmery air snaking down from a boy that lingered just long enough.

I whisper, 'Thank you, Jimi-Luke'.

And I climb. I see another ladder and I climb that too. I hear Austin behind me and we'll keep on going, up and up and up.

ALSO BY PATRICE LAWRENCE

'A TRULY BRILLIANT BOOK'
Malorie Blackman

COSTA BOOK AWARDS
2016

ORANGEBOY
PATRICE LAWRENCE
Winner of the YA Book Prize 2017

Winner of the *Waterstones Children's
Book Prize for Older Fiction*

Winner of the *Crime Fest Award for Best Crime Novel for Young Adults*

'A TRULY BRILLIANT BOOK'
Malorie Blackman on *Orangeboy*

INDIGO DONUT

PATRICE LAWRENCE

Winner of the YA Book Prize 2017

'A red-hot mystery' *The Times*

COMING IN JULY 2019

ROSE, INTERRUPTED

The brand-new novel from
award-winning author
PATRICE LAWRENCE

Hodder
Children's
Books

PATRICE LAWRENCE

was born in Brighton and brought up in an Italian-Trinidadian household in Mid Sussex. This meant great holidays and even better food. Patrice lives in east London and shares a cat called Stormageddon. She has been writing for as long as she has been reading. She loves crime fiction, sci-fi and trying to grow things. Her ideal mixtape includes drum 'n' bass, Bruce Springsteen and music from Studio Ghibli films. Music can't help creeping into her books.

 @LawrencePatrice

 facebook.com/patriceLawrence.author

patricelawrence.wordpress.com

Read on for an extract from *Colour Me In*,
the brilliant new YA novel from Lydia Ruffles …

WHAT IF WE GOT LOST TOGETHER?

COLOUR
ME IN
LYDIA
RUFFLES

'Remember the name LYDIA RUFFLES'
STYLIST

A couple of hours, some tea and a significant portion of the city by foot later, Arlo has worked up the nerve to ask Mizuki why she agreed to get a drink with him.

'Isn't this what people do when they're travelling? Meet another human in a hostel or staring at tree porn then hang out with them for a while?'

'Seriously?'

'I don't know. Maybe you looked sort of familiar.'

He can't tell her he thought the same because it'll sound like a lie now.

'And you looked a bit lost,' she adds. 'How long are you here for?'

'Not sure yet. You?'

'I'm here until fall; hopefully I'm meeting someone then going home,' she says. 'Did you come for the blossom?'

'It was an accident.'

There was an accident.

'I'm not into this spring madness.'

Now that Mizuki says it, Arlo knows he saw something about it in a magazine on the plane. It's a special time of year here, and then again in autumn when the leaves turn red, like she said. He's lucky to have caught the blossom. Perfect timing, the lady in the park had told him, as if he'd planned any of this.

Mizuki carries on, 'I lived here from when I was two until I was seven. This is my first time back in the country.'

'You seem at home,' Arlo says.

'I've been here a couple of months.'

'How come you moved away?'

'My dad's parents got sick. I don't think my mum wanted to leave but what could she do.'

They're in some older streets now. They pass a row of teahouses with tidy rows of shoes outside. *Don't they get stolen?* Arlo imagines the people inside, napping on mats. They wonder about getting more tea but decide to buy some fruit instead.

Mizuki chooses an apple, a process she takes very seriously. They get some pears, two oranges, and Arlo adds a bag of cherries. He pays to say thank you for her tour-guiding. It's expensive.

'You can get square watermelons here. They cost thousands of dollars. And giant strawberries,' Mizuki tells him.

'Why would you want a square melon?'

'Why wouldn't you?'

They find a quiet bench to share some of the oranges before continuing their walk.

A bee beats its wings at his side.

Mizuki translates a sign. 'They make honey up on the roof here.'

At school there always seemed to be insects everywhere, things with too many legs behind the radiators, buzzing at windows.

'I've never been to this part of town before,' she says.

'Don't look at me, I'm new here.' Though he's already starting to get a sense of the shape of this part of the city, connecting together in his mind all the neighbourhoods he's seen so far.

Mizuki stops to look in a shop window full of antique maps and globes. Star charts for mariners.

'Let's go in,' he says.

She follows him.

A huge antique atlas is spread over a lectern. For a second, he's in the back seat of a car in the dark. Mum at the wheel, Luke by his side. Big pages hang over the sides of his lap like wings or the curves on an anchor. A magic book for flying away, instructions for finding your path. Maybe his mum knows what happened to the lost atlas. He'll ask her.

'Useless,' Mizuki says, spinning the top of an old globe.

'Harsh.'

'The world doesn't look like that any more. Bits have broken off and parts have melted.'

Ribs crack in Arlo's ears as, somewhere, great slabs of ice and earth slide away from their homes.

He lays his hand on the globe to still it. It's room temperature. He presses, feels a pulse of pain, but isn't sure if it's him or the world that hurts.

Back out on the street, he asks Mizuki if she's a student.

'I'm an environmentalist.'

'Cool.'

'Do you know what that means?'

'Of course.' Though now that she's said it he's not sure he does. 'Did you always want to be one?' he asks.

She shakes her head. 'What did you want to be when you were a kid?'

'An actor.'

She laughs.

'Why is that funny?'

'I don't know. Just the idea of you wanting all that attention seems kind of wrong.'

It's not about wanting attention.

It's about making something that matters, connecting.

Escaping monochrome.

'What did you want to be?' he asks.

'First I wanted to be a pony. Then a doctor and a mum.'

'But you became an environmentalist.'

Mizuki lifts her camera to zoom in on a zigzag crack in the pavement. Takes a photo, checks it, deletes it. Arlo stares at the split stone; it looks like the remnants of a tiny earthquake.

'For now. What did you become or are you still becoming?'

'I'm a student,' he says, then changes the subject. 'Do you know where we are?'

'Nope.'

'Me neither.'

They cut through a botanical garden. The signs are all written in multiple languages.

'*No jogging or running in the park*,' reads Mizuki. 'There's an order I can get on board with.'

Arlo hasn't run since before the roof. That's not true; he's run eight thousand kilometres away from home.

'Should we ask someone for directions?' he says.

'I usually just keep walking if I'm lost. Eventually you'll hit a bus stop or a subway station, or something more interesting.'

She's right. They find a subway station five minutes later.

'Where are you staying?'

He tells her the name of the hotel.

'This station will work.'

He follows her underground feeling as if he were in *Alice's Adventures in Wonderland*.

Two minutes until the next train. Underground minutes always seem longer than above-ground minutes. His heart ticks along with invisible clocks. After precisely two minutes, a train pulls into the platform, slamming out a tunnel-shaped train of air first. All around the network, ghost trains are shunted along by metal tubes with seats in them.

The motion bounces their shoulders together as they sit down. Contact. Arlo shifts in case it's making Mizuki uncomfortable. She smells of fruit.

The aluminium surfaces and poles are so clean they're almost lilac in the white light; it's like being inside a UV tube. The carriage is quiet except for the automated announcements and the sounds that play in the stations as they pass – *Is that electronic birdsong?*

Both slump back in their seats, tired from their long walk. Mizuki folds her hands in her lap, twisting the engagement ring round and round. Arlo notices her silver bracelet and the charms dangling off it – two cherries, an old-fashioned camera, a leaf. He can't see what's hanging on the underside. His fingers toy with the hygiene mask in his pocket, coiling and releasing the strap.

They sweep along under the city in easy quiet. Nobody tries to take his picture. The rails don't screech.

Mizuki flicks through the photos on her camera. She favourites the ones she took lying on the ground looking up through the two twisted trees and deletes the rest.

'Yours is the next stop.'

Arlo has under half a minute to ask what he wants to ask. 'Would you . . . would you maybe want to meet up again tomorrow?' Before she can decline, he adds, 'On three?'

She puts a hand behind her back and counts, 'One, two, three.'

His paper beats her rock. Until now he'd always thought it was kind of stupid that a piece of paper could defeat a rock but he wasn't going to disagree with the rock, paper, scissors gods now.

'Do you want to put your number in my phone?' he asks.

'I've lost mine. I'll meet you at your hotel at nine a.m.'

He gives her the name again. 'You want me to write it down for you?'

'I can remember two words,' she says, 'especially when one of them is "Hotel".'

He likes the way she teases him; it's not mean and makes a change from all the people at home who try to suck up to him.

The train pulls into the station. Arlo pushes himself to his feet and yawns.

'That means you need oxygen,' Mizuki tells him. 'Or you're scared.'

'Just tired.'

'Jetlag or can't sleep?'

'Both.'

'They have a proverb here: "If you can't sleep it's because you're awake in someone else's dream."'

Arlo is pleased with his response, 'Well, if you see me in one of yours, tell me to go back to bed.'

He gives her the rest of the cherries and gets off the train.

Colour Me In **is out now in paperback and ebook.**

READING IS POWER

- What's the **GREATEST BOOK** you've ever read, the most **POWERFUL STORY** ever told?

- Which **AUTHOR** speaks to you the loudest, who is the **CHARACTER** that **STUCK IN YOUR HEAD** long after you put the book down?

- Which **ILLUSTRATORS** enchant you and make you want to pick up a pen yourself?

- How do you get your **BOOKISH** fix? Downloaded to your phone or do you prefer the feel of a book in your hands?

How do *you* share stories?

Here at World Book Day, **we celebrate books in all their glory and guises**, we love to **think and talk about books**. Did you know we are a **charity**, here to bring books, your favourite **authors and illustrators** and much more to readers like you?

We believe **BOOKS AND READING ARE A GIFT**, and this book is our gift to **YOU**.

#ShareAStory today, in celebration of all the books you love

WORLD
**BOOK
DAY**

SPONSORED BY
**NATIONAL
BOOK
tokens**

#ReadingisPower

Whatever the time of day, morning, noon or night, there's always time to discover and share stories. You can . . .

1 PAY A VISIT to your LOCAL BOOKSHOP

A treasure trove of books to browse and choose, you'll also find excellent tips and reading recommendations from helpful booksellers, and lots of book-themed events to enjoy.

FIND YOUR LOCAL BOOKSHOP: booksellers.org.uk/ bookshopsearch

2 JOIN your LOCAL LIBRARY

So many books to browse and borrow – entirely for free! Get advice on what to read next, and take part in their brilliant free activities.

FIND YOUR LOCAL LIBRARY: gov.uk/local-library -services/

3 GO TO the WORLD BOOK DAY WEBSITE

If you need inspiration, reading and writing tips, ideas or resources, **worldbookday.com** is packed with fun and exciting podcasts, videos, activities, interviews with your favourite authors and illustrators, all the latest book news and much more.

Celebrate stories. Love reading.